For my great friend Lorna and her beautiful daughters. C.W.

For my delightfully noisy nibblers, Lori and Jamie. R.B.

American edition published in 2013 by Andersen Press USA,
an imprint of Andersen Press Ltd.
www.andersenpressusa.com

First published in Great Britain in 2013 by Andersen Press Ltd.,
20 Vauxhall Bridge Road, London SW1V 2SA.
Published in Australia by Random House Australia Pty.,
Level 3, 100 Pacific Highway, North Sydney, NSW 2060.

Distributed in the United States and Canada by
Lerner Publishing Group, Inc.
241 First Avenue North
Minneapolis, MN 55401 U.S.A.
www.lernerbooks.com

Color separated in Switzerland by Photolitho AG, Zürich.
Printed and bound in Malaysia by Tien Wah Press.

Library of Congress Cataloging-in-Publication Data Available.
ISBN: 978-1-4677-2032-8
ISBN: 978-1-4677-2038-0 (eBook)

1 - TWP - 3/27/13

FSC
www.fsc.org

MIX
Paper from
responsible sources
FSC® C012700

What Noise Does a Rabbit Make?

Written by **Carrie Weston**

Illustrated by **Richard Byrne**

ANDERSEN PRESS USA

In the still of the night,
    just before dawn,
        slowly and silently . . .

. . . the meadow filled
with rabbits.

Raggety-Taggle
and his brothers
and his sisters,
his aunts,
and his uncles,
all nibbled peacefully.

But as the sun came up . . .

Cock-a-doodle-do!

trumpeted the rooster.

Moo!

went the cows.

Neigh!

said the horses.

Baa-baaaaaaaaa!

the sheep joined in.

Oink! Oink!

grunted the pigs.

Tweet Tweet

Meow!

went the cat in search
of her breakfast.

Woof!
Woof!

barked the dog as the farmer
started his tractor.

Chu-chu-brrr-chug,
chug, chug!

The farm rang out with noises.

Raggety-Taggle listened with his long ears and thought very hard.

Tweet Tweet

"Just what noise **does** a rabbit make?"

he wondered.

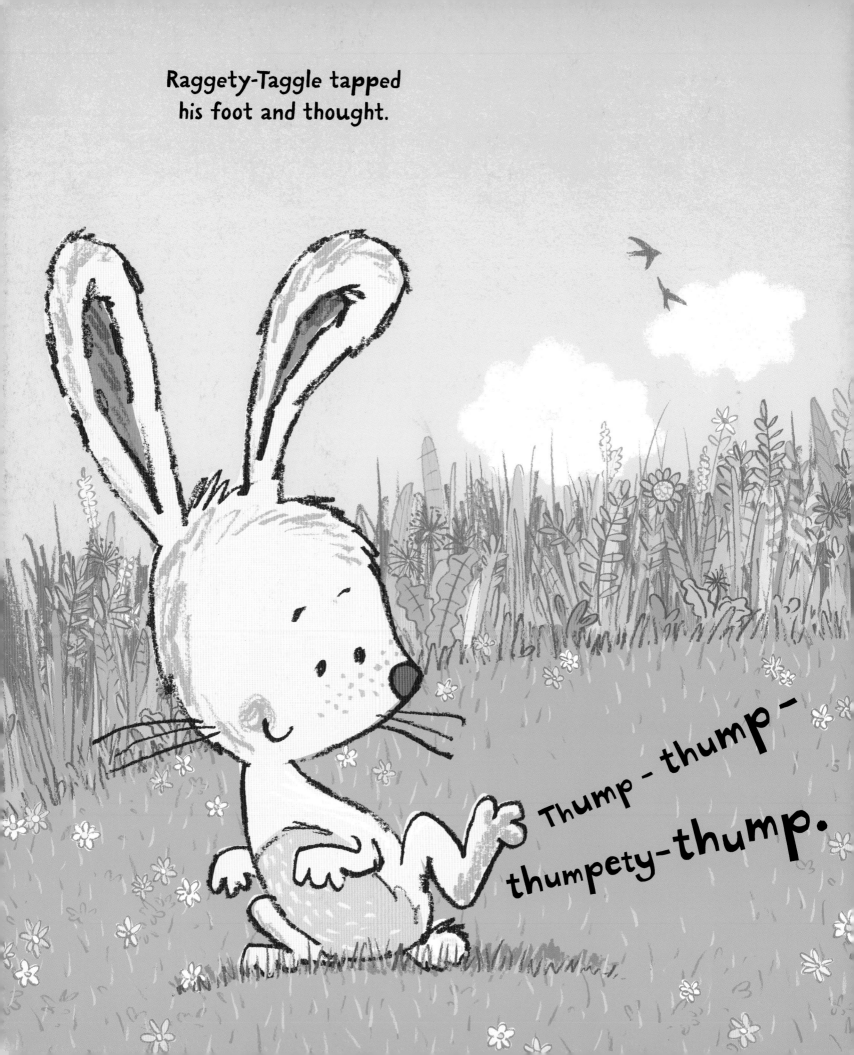

Raggety-Taggle tapped
his foot and thought.

Thump - thump - thumpety-thump.

A long way off,
   in the tall grass,
      two ears pricked up.
         A tail flicked.

Two eyes blinked.

Whiskers twitched.
   The cat licked her lips.

Thump - thump -
thumpety - thump!

went Raggety-Taggle.

He didn't see that
the other rabbits had
swiftly, silently,
disappeared into their burrows.

The cat crouched.
The cat wriggled.

The cat . . .

pounced!

MIAOW!
Hiss!

Raggety-Taggle
ran
for
his
life.

Through the cow field,

Mooo
oOooO
Oooooo!

over the sheep pen,

Baa-baaaa!

round the stables,

Neeeeeeeigh!

under the pigs,

OINK! OINK!

and right past the dog.

WOOF! WOOF!

Then as the cat
        chased after Raggety-Taggle . . .

. . . the dog chased after the cat . . .

WOOF!

MIAOW!

. . . followed by the cows, Moo!

then the sheep, Baa-baaaa!

the horses, Neigh!

the pigs, Oink! Oink!

with the rooster flapping behind . . .

Cock-a-doodle-do!

The angry farmer blew the tractor horn,

TOOT!

and everybody . . .

stopped.

All, that is, except for Raggety-Taggle,

who quietly tucked up his tail . . .

and ran . . .

and ran . . .

and ran . . .

all the way home.

Later that evening, as the sun went down
and the farmyard grew quiet,
slowly and silently . . .
the meadow filled with rabbits.

Raggety-Taggle nibbled peacefully
and wondered just why **anybody**
would **ever** want to make
a noise **at all.**